The Magician and The Vampire King

Written by Zoli Althea Browne

Illustrated by Bob D'Amico

Preface

The Reality Pirate (RP) skidded to a stop, dropping his spyglass like a hot potato.

The dim light of two moons swallowed the castle drowning in sublime angelic dust. But what was that? Did a white horse just block his view of the Lion's Gate portal?

RP was tired. Enough of this mystical-shymistical drama. All he wanted was a full belly and a nice nap away from anything breathing. And yes, that actually was a horse on the castle lawn.

Retrieving his spyglass from the moat's edge, RP sighed, attempting to focus on the scene unfolding twenty yards away. But who was that walking slowly from the portal towards the horse? As the mist cleared, RP recognized the traditional robes and hat of a sorcerer gently grasping the horse's reins as it lifted its magnificent head to face RP.

The white horse shimmered in the moonlight; its eyes fixed upon the squat form of this alien intruder. RP shifted uncomfortably, imagining the horse secreting powers and spells capable of ruining his day. And to make it worse, RP now observed an elf carrying a clay jug, drunkenly stumbling from the forest into a ditch. It managed to pick itself up, retrieve its jug of whatever and continue towards the castle. God, he hated it here. Magicians and drunk elves were out of his comfort zone. But right now, his comfort zone was a snack and some damn privacy.

RP squinted into the spyglass while trying to remember why he fell into this planet's atmosphere in the first place. Was this a time portal or a place portal?

Hc seemed to recall some magician lecturing a young RP on the inherent differences between finding oneself in a different

time or a different place but in the same time. He fingered the Returnometer in his pocket and wondered if he'd returned to someone else's life.

Now, he was getting a headache. He'd not eaten anything since leaving Mme Oracular's Common Café on Zanzibar Prime. RP set down the spyglass and dug around in his other pocket for a Bully Bar. You know, the pressed cowhide flavored with Demetria Mallow? I'm sure you've had one.

But no such luck. By now, he could see the castle more clearly with those two moons melting from the orange sun of the Ambrosia system. He hated this.

WTF was he doing here? Had he fallen into a food coma after his par-tay and forgot to set the économètre to the Spica system? I mean, Spica is ten times the size of Earth, so how the hell did he mcss this up?

RP plopped down onto the grass and tried to focus.

Landing on an unknown planet with mystical characters was damn near irresponsible. He tried to remember what the Gnostic Gnomes had revealed to him about these potential synchronicities, but all he could remember was that part about going with the flow and not adding

emotion to the situation. Well, he was already emotional, and you can just forget about the damn flow shit. RP sighed and rummaged around again for at least a half-eaten something, but still no luck. He'd have to Zen it, just calm down, and focus.

The castle glimmered with morning dew, gracing the verdant landscape with a beauty RP recalled from his travels in the Vega planetary areas. He sighed and sat back down, waiting for something to happen.

"Please let something interesting happen to tell me why I'm here," he mused.

A horn sounded in the distance. It was the kind of horn sound you'd expect to announce something happening, not just some random bleep from a trumpet. RP stood up and pressed his spyglass to his eye. That elf, you know, that one, was running like a banshee towards the white circus-looking tent, feet flopping and tripping whenever it looked behind to see who was following. But no one was.

"This is weird," said RP to no one in particular. As he watched the drunken elf, he felt a presence behind him before jerking around to see the white magician peering down at him. RP stole one more look at the elf before turning to face the tall, regal figure who seemed to bear the presence of one who'd lost something important. "Sad, that was it, he's sad."

RP relaxed a bit, relieved to think he was not in danger of being turned into a Woa-Toadie. (You remember those dudes with a turtle body and canine legs with a grinning cat smile? Very cute, from the Pleiadian Construct).

To RP's surprise, the Magician plopped down onto the still-damp grass, laying his long staff unceremoniously alongside him. The horse ambled over and sniffed his hat, indifferent to all the drama. RP mused that whoever cleaned those white robes for him was going to be big-pissed. The purple grass on this planet was going to leave.

"Wha'd you say?" The Magician's kind voice broke the silence. "Did you just say something about my robe?"

Oh great, thought RP. This ancient dude can read my mind.

Adjusting his robes so he could pull his knees into a kid position, the Magician stared at RP, as curious about him as RP was about the Magician.

"So, I'll start," said the purple-stained-robe dude. "I came here 264 years ago just to get a little R and R from the rabble-rousers on Pluto. They are idiots, but I'd promised the Council I'd see what I could do, you know, to seek out one or two conscious beings among the closed-off masses. But it didn't work. I'm stuck here because of that damned elf."

RP attempted a concerned look, but squishing his eyebrows only made him look more like RP. The Magician toyed with a blade of grass while the horse sauntered off to the calm moat for a swim.

"I really didn't mean for any of this to happen," began the Magician. "Things got away from me. The Vampire King has always played by his own rules. No one can work with him, especially me. So, this is a real mess."

RP wondered what exactly the mess was but didn't want to appear dumber than he felt. The damp purple grass had stained his palms and threatened to redefine him as a local, God forbid. But who was this Vampire King, and why blame a drunk elf?

"Oh, I'll tell you," said the mind-reading Magician. "But maybe it's better if you read the story, huh? I'm tired to the bone with this. Here," he said as he handed RP a parchment scroll tied with purple ribbon.

"Take some time and see what you think. I'm heading into the castle for a bit. After shifting realities, I had to reassemble all my damn atoms just to create this 3D body, you know? It's a damn shame the Vampire King took all this so personally.

After all, it was a stupid ancient curse and a stupider ancient drama. I define this as a karmic issue between him and me. As you know, we are actually…"

"Is there food?" RP stood hurriedly, grabbing the scroll, bored with the story; he was hangry and tired. More mystical-shymistical shit. He hopped up and followed the purple robes into the castle, stumbling over a sleeping elf, cuddled in the grass next to the moat.

The Magician and the Vampire King are now revealed to you. Guard yourself, for what is real is false, and deception is the law of reality.

The Magician rinsed his eyes with dew, stretching out a craggy hand to test the earliness of the day, only to withdraw it in terror. The vintage was gone, consumed in the smugness of night.

"Ah! Damned elf! Spiteful creature she is. The Vampire King shall surely revoke my powers now that the sacred protection is drunk!"

(She swore she'd never touched the wine, and curled her fingers like a child, sleeping her dreamless void-of-a sleep with nothing more to offer.) Morning presented itself, devoid of feeling for the Sage.

The Vampire King broke fast. The ravaged harlot reposed in his chamber.

The Magician raccooned around his tent, writhing in vengeance. The victory spoilt as the elf sputtered taxingly in her sleep, flushed of cheek and bloated stomach, she slept.

And the whiteness of the horse stepped respectfully towards the tent of his master.

Integrity pooled in his velvet eyes, sensing as such creatures will sense, a sorrowful air of blackness, curtailing the tent from the perfume of dawn.

Pressing into his memory, the Magician bent over his dusty Grimoire, remorseful and uncertain, hoping only for a sweet victory to come. Where was the title bestowed upon him by that ancient, vintage master?

Curiously, cautiously, the Magician mounded his thoughts, like the rich sod, softening under the hooves of his horse. Carefully teaching his swollen anger to focus only on his precious book of magic.

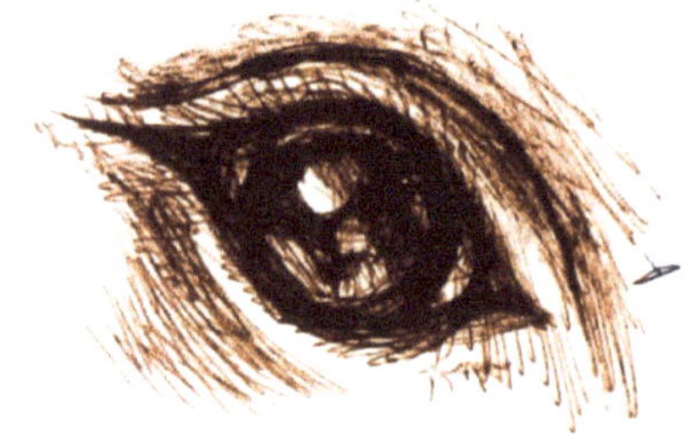

Life forms of all varieties pulled themselves through the folds of the tent, drawn magnetically to the mournful saga of the wasted vintage. (Trusted elf, her irascible precociousness, a bad marriage within the Magician's heart!)

Eons of responsibility weighed precariously in his hands.

His bearded figure trusting the celebrated pages, comforted by their

proximity, yet grieved with the loss, of a solution to his misery.

(And the white horse tossed his head into the rarified air, posed

above the poisoned tent, seeking celestial shelter, scented with

the promise of hope.)

Seductive life forms crackled

under the weight of that

heaviness. The horse revived,

returned dutifully to the gaze of his Master, committing to a long sleep, the polite

silence of the Sage.

Morning, embarrassed by her tardiness, crackled into a bright noon. Still, the Magician scratched through the depths of his mind for the moment,

yes, the very moment he lost touch with that

damned elf, the wine cellar unguarded

and vulnerable.

Pouring over the sacred writings.

Retracing each step. Tearing at his hands

with bloodied nails, he pained through,

those crackled pages until there...there was a sentence resting alone on the bottom

of a page, yes. There, beneath his stale gaze lay the key to his horror, the hubris of

his dement.

"So, tell me now your life is planned," it began.

(He turned the cracked page.)

"That words I speak won't lend a hand. Protect the wine, or you'll be damned,

to fight eternal tears." The vintage words spoken long ago by the Vampire King

whispered in the twin breaths of creation. "The love of my forgotten soul, betrayed by foolish pride

and sold, with blackened sheets on dismal roads, lay bloody, foul, and weak."

The Magician's hand shook as he turned those antique pages. Memories of what was, melded with the stark reality of what he wished it were not. "And o'er the mist and dying moon, I rose to shed my cloak of doom, to steal unnoticed to your room, and watch the dagger sink."

Black reveries starkly contrasted the crisp freshness of noonday air. A timeless story of the Vampire King and his Magician, of how he had elevated the Sage with untold powers, the only return was to protect the sacred vintage.

"So, tell me now your life is planned? The worlds you seek can lend no hand. Your failure now has left you damned, to fight eternal tears!"

The Magician recoiled in terror, flinging the book onto the warm sand in the tent. His salvation from the Vampire King lay mounding in the swollen gut of that damned elf.

The Vampire King would destroy the Magician; his powers, weaving his being into the rank fabric of a dead eternity. The lifeforms transformed themselves in the ether. The white horse breathed a silent breath. Evening edged its dusk into the arms of the terrified Magician.

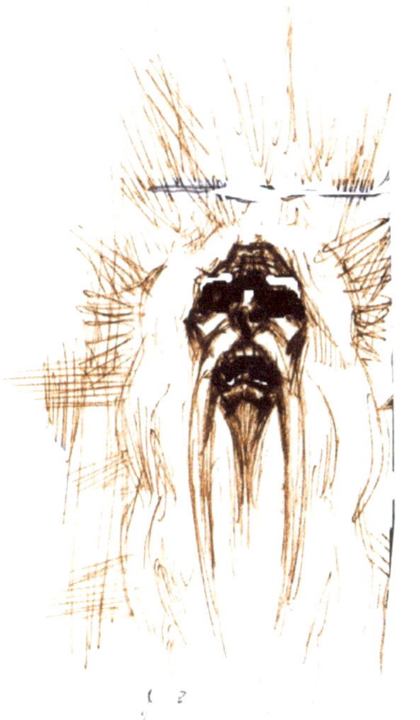

Magic lifted; the Sage dropped into the pillows of his tent. Stripped to a neophyte rank, he lay beaten and sobbing. The ground beneath him began to shake. The stone table cradling the great book cracked and covered him with debris. A great wind arose from the terrible depths, spraying marble dust into a whirlwind, forming in the vortex. The Magician reached a weakened hand towards the sacred book but fell back into the wind as it lifted the book high

above his head, above the torn tent and into the

outstretched arms of the Vampire King!

Hesitating now, between shifting realities,

anticipating the final transformation, the corporeal

structure of the tent folded into the dense cloud,

dropping

into the

black void in the Earth.

The Magician, weakened and jaded, floated above the chasm,

naked in the crosswinds. The mind of the Vampire King

supported the darkness, striking the Magician with torturous

energy. Round and round, he spun his prey, the physical body

tearing flesh and bone, all physicality did dilate into the

atoms of those lands in between.

Ethers. Melted forms whooshing past his consciousness, the Magician entered that nebulous world with the Vampire King. And now, in the coolness of a black moonless night, the unsuspecting elf rose from her inebriated slumber, suppliant with hope for an evening of play.

(She'd found the key but lost the lock; what good?)

And curling her fingers like a child, she grasped the cool crock of vintage,

swallowing down the final drops with nothing more to offer.

"So, tell me now your life was planned! The worlds you seek won't lend a hand.

Your lies to me have left us damned, to fight eternal tears."

Fini

This terribly dark poem was written on January 19, 1980, at Carolyn Shield's condo in Washington, DC. The rainy day found me gazing at her large, ornate coffee table book, *The Rubaiyat* by Omar Khayyam. The opening etching displayed a sage-looking man gently bending over a sleeping child. I then found myself in a different density, tranced out with this poem pressing me to write all I felt.

The poem "To Fight Eternal Tears" was written by me in 1972 while remaining in L'Auberge de Noves due to illness. I will reveal this story in Reinerio Hernandez's upcoming consciousness book on experiences.

When I channeled the "Magician Poem," this poem fell into place alongside the storyline. Things work like this sometimes.

About Us

Zoli Althea Browne is an author, musician, and artist who lives in a castle in the mountains of Montana where she is visited by RP and other supernatural beings. Her poem, the Magician and the Vampire King became an unlikely adventure for the Reality Pirate (RP).

Bob D'Amico of CartoonBob Studios is the artist who brought this story to life. As an illustrator and cartoonist, he also has years of experience as a New York City creative and art director. He can be reached at:

Dedicated to all the magical hearts and minds. May your love for magic and realms unknown inspire you to new adventures. Go in Peace. – Zoli Althea

Coming soon another RP adventure!